P9-ARQ-531

I Am Smart
A POSITIVE POWER STORY

by Suzy Capozzi

illustrated by Eren Unten

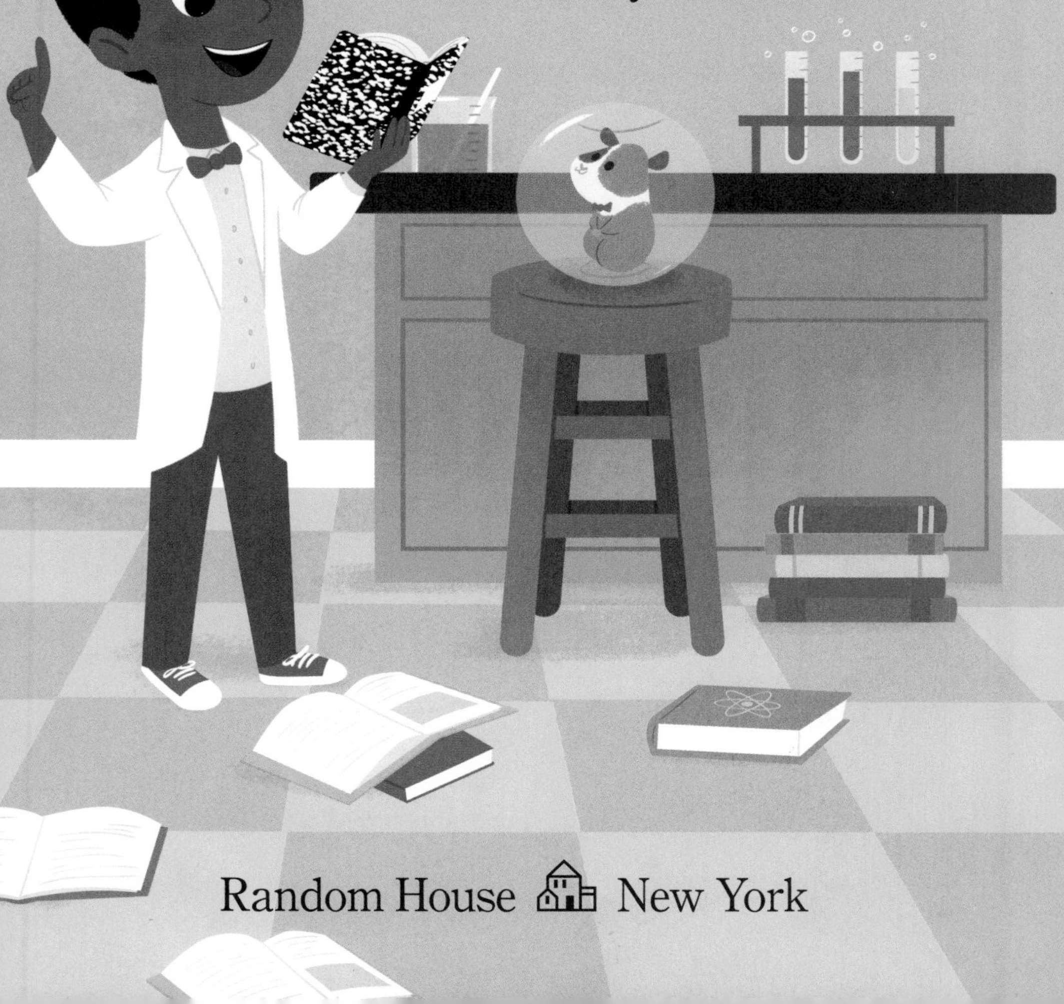

Random House 🏠 New York

My alarm clock
wakes me up.
I get dressed and
go downstairs.

Mom made
my favorite breakfast—
egg-in-a-hole.
I am too nervous to eat.
I need to study.

I have a math test,
and one more review
will make me feel better.

Mom says, "You studied
last night. You got
a good night's sleep.
Now it's time
for brain food."

Mom is right!
I am prepared.
Now I am fueled up
and ready to go.
Breakfast was
a smart choice.

I am smart.
I've got this covered!

I feel hopeful all day
until science class.
Our teacher makes
an announcement.
We will have a science
fair in two weeks.

I do not like science.
It is hard for me.
I worry about the fair
in gym class.

I worry about it
all the way home.

I am *still* worrying
about it at night.
Mom knows I struggle
in science class.
She encourages me
to pick something
I like or do every day.

"Look for the science in your life," she says.

And just like that,
I get an idea.
It's a good idea.
It's a smart idea!

I jot down some notes
before I go to sleep.
I have so many questions.

I go to the library on Saturday.
First, I look up
information on my own.

Next, I ask the librarian.
"You ask very smart
questions," he says.

Over the next few days,
I read about gravity and
how it flips a bottle.
I learn how weight,
shape, and speed
affect the bottle.

I make a lot of noise and
it gets a little messy.

Then I spend a few days
trying different setups.
I add different amounts
of water to the bottles.

I try bigger bottles
and smaller bottles.
Chance and Taylor stop by.
They want to play soccer.

But I don't want to
stop working on my experiment.
My experiment is fun.
I show my friends.
I ask them for help.

They stay and have fun.
I made a smart choice.

Our teacher gives us permission to work together!

We record the results.

We make posters.

WATER

We practice doing demonstrations.

Finally, the science fair is here.
I am nervous and excited.
We answer everyone's
questions.

Our experiment works!

THE EFFECT OF
DIFFERENT WATER
AMOUNTS USED FOR
BOTTLE FLIPPING

It is time
to hand out prizes.
Chance, Taylor, and I
cross our fingers
and link arms.

We win a prize
for best demonstration.
We flip out!

I worked hard.
I asked for help.
Chance, Taylor, and I
celebrate with sundaes.

I learned a lot
about bottle flipping,
science, and myself.
I am smart.

For the always insightful Danny
—S.C.

To Wayne, Emily, and Amelia
—E.U.

Text copyright © 2018 by Suzy Capozzi
Cover art and interior illustrations copyright © 2018 by Eren Unten

All rights reserved. Published in the United States by Random House Children's Books, a division of Penguin Random House LLC, New York. Originally published by Rodale Kids, an imprint of Random House Children's Books, a division of Penguin Random House LLC, New York, in 2018.

Step into Reading, Random House, and the Random House colophon are registered trademarks of Penguin Random House LLC.

Visit us on the Web!
rhcbooks.com

Educators and librarians, for a variety of teaching tools, visit us at RHTeachersLibrarians.com

Library of Congress Cataloging-in-Publication Data is available upon request.
ISBN 978-0-593-56490-5 (trade) — ISBN 978-0-593-56491-2 (lib. bdg.) —
ISBN 978-0-593-56492-9 (ebook)

Printed in the United States of America
10 9 8 7 6 5 4 3 2 1

This book has been officially leveled by using the F&P Text Level Gradient™ Leveling System.